Linden —

Hope you enjoy a
this story about a
little longhorn. From your
Texas 'family.

Love you,
Amanda & Walter
Feb 2015

BODIE

&

THE BURNT ORANGE SUNSET

BY RICK KING

ILLUSTRATED BY MARIO RIVERA

Lone Star Publishing
Houston 2010

ISBN 9781589808751

Designed by Miguel A. Martinez and Daniela Fishburn

Special Creative Consultant: Charlie Moore

Bodie's first baby photo. Liberty Hill, Texas.

Printed in Singapore
Published by Lone Star Publishing, L.L.C.
5220 Caroline Suite 9, Houston, Texas 77004

For my parents, who met at The University of Texas

Special gratitude to Sally Brown for her tireless
support of greater causes, Coach Brown for lighting
the tower burnt orange once again, and
Coach Royal for blazing the trail

Deep in the heart of Texas,
there's a story to hear—
a heartwarming tale
'bout Bodie the steer.

Not so long ago,
in a barn filled with hay,
a momma cow waited
all the livelong day.

Then there in that barn,
as the summer sun set,
baby Bodie arrived—
a day we shan't forget.

"A treasure he is!"
His proud papa beamed.
Even the heavens smiled,
or so it did seem.

For right then the sky
did something amazin'.
Suddenly, everywhere,
burnt orange was a-blazin'!

"Burnt orange," they all whispered
as they looked on in awe.
"You know what that means!"
bellowed Bodie's proud pa.

Tiny Bodie, he shouted,
"I'm gonna be famous!"
The other calves mooed,
"You're a runt ignoramus!"

They pointed and jeered,
they had such a ball.
"And heck," they all snorted,
"you're not three feet tall!"

But Bodie knew better—
he'd grow big and grow strong.
So he set out to prove
all the naysayers wrong.

Crossing fields of bright green
and rivers of blue,
he traveled for days
and the darkest nights, too.

He yapped and he yapped
and chased Bodie away.
But Bodie thought, "Good golly, Collie,
I'll be back one day."

Down the road Bodie passed
a toothless ol' coot,
who was drivin' his wagon
with a hollerin' hoot.

He spurred on his wagon
with a look of disgust,
leaving Bodie behind
with a snout full of dust.

Bodie trekked on and on
and spied a bear in the trees.
That silly ol' bear
had green socks to his knees.

That bear in green socks
growled, snarled, and spit.
That bear in green socks
charged Bodie in a snit.

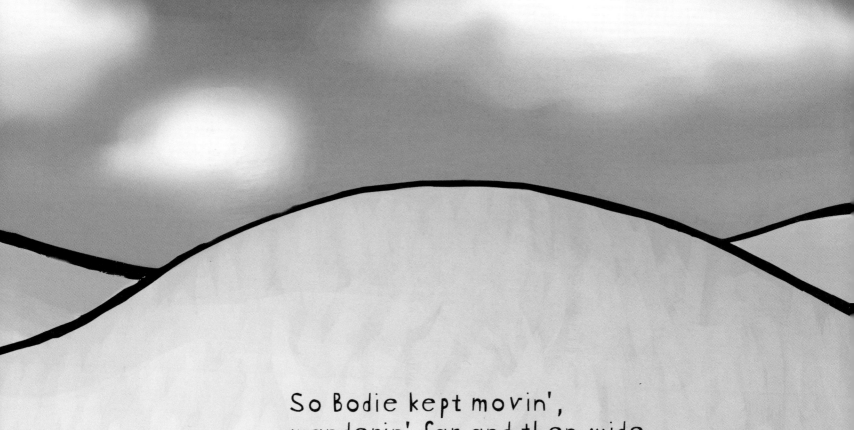

So Bodie kept movin',
wanderin' far and then wide,
and in the high plains
found a place to reside.

Now Bodie knew good fortune
wasn't given away.
If he wanted fame,
he must train night and day.

Through acres of grain,
he chomped, chewed, and ate.
His chest kept on growing;
his horns, they grew great.

Then early one morn
while asleep on his bed,
masked men came on horseback,
raiding in red.

Bodie heard 'em a-comin'
and kicked up a storm.
And in that tornado,
his legend was born.

Those horsemen paid dearly
for disturbing his snores,
and with that Bodie set out
to settle old scores.

He found that bear's tree
and he shook and he shook.
That ol' bear learned quickly
that horns do hook!

Later he found that wagon,
stuck in a rut by the road.
Bodie gave him a big old nudge
to help lighten his load.

Then Bodie stepped out
on that collie's lush lawn.
And he didn't stop grazin'
'til the grass was all gone.

The news traveled fast,
from near to afar.
Back home at the ranch,
he'd become quite a star.

He now lives in Austin
with his Horn fans galore.
His story's a legend,
the stuff of folklore.

If you want to meet him,
just go to a game.
When you see that proud beef,
just call out his name.

You've probably guessed
who li'l Bodie became.
Yes, Bodie and Bevo
are one and the same.

HOOK 'EM HORNS!

Do You Know the Real Bevo?

Since 1966, Bevo, a true Texas longhorn, has been a fixture at University of Texas (UT) football games.

The longhorn was an important part of building the American West. Brought to North America by Spanish explorers, the breed flourished for nearly five hundred years. It was the toughest, leanest breed of cattle and could survive when other types of cattle could not. Cattlemen have great respect for the tenacity of the Texas longhorn.

Longhorns are durable and independent and can grow to weigh a ton or more. Their horns can span six to nine feet.

UT chose the Texas longhorn to be its mascot in the early 1900s, because of its toughness, strength, and determination to survive against all odds in harsh conditions.

Longhorns serve as "Bevo" for many years. The longest reign was of Bevo XIII, who was at the presidential inauguration of George W. Bush in Washington, D.C.

Bevo has his own air-conditioned trailer and is cared for by the Silver Spurs Association.

Today, all Bevos are retired to live out the rest of their years on the ranches where they grew up.

Bevo is the heaviest of all mammal mascots, and his likeness is used as the famous UT emblem.

A Special Thanks

Special thanks to the passionate people who made this story possible: Daniela Fishburn; Sally Brown; Mom and Dad; Shawn, John, August, and Gillian Fricker; Charlie and Kari Moore; Kirk Gills; Craig Westemeier; Ricky Brennes; Milburn Calhoun; Nina Kooij; Sally Boitnott; Terry and Nancy King; John Adams; Megan Dahlstrom; Bill Broyles; Mike Novak; Vince Young; Marjorie King; Tina Houston; Greg Lofgren; Miguel Martinez; Ross Mansfield; John Burpeau; Bill Hinkle; John T. Baker; Sam LaRue; Texas Exes; Lyndon Baines Johnson Library and Museum; South Texas Longhorn Association; all Bevos and loyal Longhorns everywhere, . . . and, of course, Lori too.

Hook 'Em!

GO!

HORNS

GO!

HORNS

GO!

HORNS

GO!